David the Rebel

叛逆大維打工記

Coleen Reddy　著
倪靖、郜欣、王平　繪
蘇秋華　譯

三民書局

In Memory of Pat

The Granny with a dry sense of humor!

謹以此書紀念 Pat——

我那堪稱是冷面笑匠的外婆!

It's tough being thirteen years old. David knew all about that. His big problem was MONEY. He needed money and he needed lots of it. A thirteen-year-old can't survive without money. His parents always said he WANTED money, but that wasn't true. He NEEDED money.

10%

He needed money to buy clothes. His parents bought him clothes, but they bought boring clothes that he was embarrassed to wear. His mom still bought him Pikachu underwear! He also needed money to go to the movies. Right now though, he needed money for something else.

Valentine's Day was next week, and he needed to get a Valentine's gift for Amy Smith. Amy Smith was his friend, and he really liked her. He wanted to buy her a Valentine's Day card, a box of expensive chocolates, and a cute teddy bear. Girls liked that sort of thing. They loved gifts. Amy was sure to love his gifts. Maybe she would even love him a little.

He didn't have any money because he had spent his allowance on a pair of jeans. He had to ask his parents for more money. His father was like Mr. Scrooge. He would have to beg for the money.

"*Dad, I need some money,*" *said David.*

"*You mean that you WANT some money,*" *said his father.*

"*No, I NEED it for something important,*" *said David.*

"*What do you need the money for, David?*" *asked his dad.*

David couldn't really tell his dad that he needed money to buy Amy a Valentine's gift. That would be too embarrassing and his father wouldn't understand. He would probably say that David was too young to be thinking about girls...blah, blah, blah...

"I just need it, Dad. Come on. You're my father. I'm your son. You're supposed to give me money," said David.

"I'll give you money if you tell me what it's for," said his dad.

"I can't, Dad," said David. It didn't look like his dad was going to give him anything.

"If you can't tell me then I can't give you money. But you can EARN money," said his dad.

"What do you mean?" asked David.

"If you do some work around the house, I could pay you for it," said his dad.

"What do you want me to do?" asked David.

"The living room and the bathroom need to be painted. If you do that, I will pay you $25," said his father.

"Okay, I'll paint it next weekend after you give me the money," said David.

"No, David. Paint the rooms first, then I'll pay you," said his dad firmly.

"But it will take forever," said David.

"That's the only way that you'll get money out of me," said his father.

"That's not fair," said David.

"Take it or leave it," said his father.

David could see that his father meant what he said. He decided to give it a try.

David put on some old, ugly clothes that he never wore anymore and started painting. He started in the living room. He worked hard. After half an hour, he was finished.

"It wasn't as hard as I thought it would be," thought David.

He called his father to take a look at his hard work. His father and mother walked into the living room. Their smiles dropped off their faces.

"Oh no!" said his mother.

"What have you done?" asked his father angrily.

"I painted the walls like you asked me to do," said David.

"You didn't do a very good job," said his father, "in fact, you've done a terrible job!"

"I don't understand," said David. What was wrong with his parents? They were never satisfied with anything.

"There are three paintings on the wall. You're supposed to remove them before you paint. You can't just paint around them," said his father.

"And you should have taken all the furniture out," said his mom, "you've dropped paint all over my expensive sofas. They're ruined!"

"I'm not paying you for this," said his father, "you have to do it again."

"No way! I am not your slave! I don't want your stupid money," said David angrily. He went to his room and slammed the door. What would he do now?

David had to get a job, but the only job he could get was delivering newspapers. He would have to do it.

The next morning, he started. He had 100 newspapers to deliver. He would use his bicycle. He started a few blocks away from his home. It was hard work.

He was supposed to throw the newspapers from his bicycle to the doorsteps. But David couldn't aim well. The newspapers landed in trees and once it even landed on the roof. But the worst was when he threw a newspaper and it hit an old man in the face. The old man yelled at him.

David stopped throwing newspapers. He got off his bicycle and put each newspaper right at each doorstep. This took a long time. It was so hot that David started sweating. Sweat was pouring down his face, down his back, and even down his legs.

His newspaper route took him to the street that Amy lived on. He hoped she didn't see him because he looked and smelt so bad. He had to deliver a newspaper to the house right next to Amy's house! He got off his bicycle and walked into the yard to deliver the newspaper. He had taken a few steps when he heard a growl. He turned around and saw a dog. It was growling at him and it had big, sharp teeth.

David was afraid of dogs. He started screaming and tried to run away but the dog was too fast. The dog barked loudly. People came out of their houses to see what was going on. Amy and her brother, Jack, also came out to look.

"Isn't that your friend David?" asked Jack.

"Yes, what is he doing?" asked Amy.

The dog had bitten into David's new, expensive jeans and was pulling them off. David screamed and tried to get free, but the dog held on tightly.
The dog pulled and pulled, and then, the most embarrassing thing happened. The dog pulled David's jeans down and left him standing there in his underwear! David couldn't believe it. The dog ran away with his jeans. He looked across and saw Amy. He was so embarrassed; he wished he could die.

"Hey David, cool underpants!" said Jack. Amy giggled. David looked down and groaned. He had forgotten. He was wearing the Pikachu underwear that his mother had bought him. It had been the worst day of his life.

An hour later, David came home. Jack had lent him a pair of pants to wear home. He felt awful.

"How did it go?" asked his dad.

He told his dad everything.

"I'm sorry, son, but what did you need the money for anyway?" asked his dad.

David decided to be honest and tell his dad that he wanted the money to buy Amy gifts for Valentine's Day.

"Oh, I see!" laughed his father, "I'll give you money for THAT."

"Really? I thought you wouldn't understand," said David.

"I was also young once and I remember what it's like," said his dad.

David looked at his dad. He couldn't picture his father as a young boy, but he was happy that his father understood. He also felt a bit stupid. If he had just told his dad the truth, he wouldn't have had such an awful day and Amy wouldn't have seen his Pikachu underwear.

David sighed. Being thirteen years old was tough. Very tough!

叛逆大維打工記

十三歲的孩子可真不好當，大維可以深切體會這句話的含意。他最大的問題就是：「錢」。他需要錢，很多的錢。一個十三歲的孩子沒有錢是無法生存的，他的爸媽總認為他「想要」錢，但他們錯了，他不是「想要」錢，而是「需要」錢。他需要錢買衣服。爸媽雖然會買衣服給他，可是他們選的都是些醜到讓他覺得穿出去很丟臉的衣服。他都那麼大了，媽媽居然還會買皮卡丘的內褲給他！他還需要錢看電影。而現在他則需要錢買東西——下個禮拜就是情人節了，大維想買個情人節禮物送愛玫・史密斯。他和愛玫是朋友，而且他很喜歡她，所以他希望能買張情人節卡片、一盒昂貴的巧克力，以及一隻可愛的泰迪熊送她。女生都喜歡這些玩意兒，她們最愛收到禮物了，所以他認為愛玫一定會喜歡他送的禮物，搞不好還會因此而愛上他呢！問題是他已經把全部財產拿去買了一條牛仔褲，所以現在是半毛錢也不剩了。他得再向爸媽要一點錢。他的爸爸是個一毛不拔的鐵公雞，大維知道他非得低聲下氣的才能幺得到一點零用錢。

(p.1～p.7)

大維說：「爸，我需要錢。」

爸爸回答：「你是說你『想要』錢吧？」

大維說：「才不是，我是真的『需要』錢，有重要的用途啦。」

爸爸質疑：「那你要錢做什麼？」

大維不想老實跟爸爸說他需要錢買情人節禮物送愛玫，這樣實在太丟臉了，而且爸爸一定不會了解。他八成會說大維年紀還小，不適合交女朋友什麼的。

所以大維說：「我就是需要錢嘛，爸爸。你是我爸爸，我是你兒子，你本來就應該給我錢的啊！」

但爸爸堅持要知道錢的用途：「如果你告訴我錢要花到哪裡去，我就給你錢。」

大維說：「不行啦，爸！」看來爸爸一分錢都不會給他。

爸爸又說：「如果你不說，我錢也不能給你。不過你可以自己賺啊。」

大維不明白：「什麼意思？」

爸爸開出條件：「如果你分攤一些家事的話，我就付錢給你。」

大維問：「那你要我做什麼？」

爸爸回答：「客廳和浴室都得重新粉刷了，如果你幫忙粉刷的話，我就給你二十五塊錢。」

(p.7～p.11)

大維說：「好吧，我下個禮拜就做，你先給我錢。」

爸爸卻絲毫不為所動：「不行，大維，你得先去漆牆壁，然後我才會付錢給你。」

大維抱怨：「可是粉刷牆壁要很久呢。」

爸爸說：「這是你唯一能從我這裡得到錢的辦法。」

大維說：「不公平。」

爸爸才不管公不公平：「隨便你囉。」

大維看得出來爸爸說到做到，只好決定先試試看再說。

大維穿上又醜又舊，以後絕對不會再穿的衣服，然後開始粉刷。他從客廳開始，埋頭努力工作，才半個小時就完成了。

他慶幸：「好像沒有我想像的困難嘛！」

（p.11～p.15）

他叫爸媽來欣賞他辛勤工作的成果。可是當爸媽一起走到客廳時，臉上的笑容卻一下子垮了下來。

媽媽說：「噢，不會吧！」

爸爸怒氣沖沖地問：「你到底做了什麼好事？」

大維很無辜：「我按照你所說的，把客廳牆壁粉刷了一遍啊。」

爸爸說：「你做的不是很好，坦白說吧，我認為牆壁被你漆得亂七八糟。」

大維說：「我不懂你的意思。」爸媽究竟怎麼了，好像不管他做什麼，他們都不會滿意。

爸爸回答：「牆上有三幅畫，你在粉刷之前應該先把它們拿下來才對，不能只沿著它們的周圍粉刷啊！」

媽媽接著說：「而且你也應該先把傢俱抬出去，你看油漆都滴到沙發上了，我花很多錢買的，現在全毀了。」

爸爸又說：「我不會付錢給你的，你得重做！」

大維氣急敗壞地抗議：「不行！我又不是個奴隸，我才不稀罕你的臭錢呢。」

他衝回房間，「碰」的一聲把門關上。

現在他該怎麼辦呢？

(p.17～p.20)

大維得去找份工作，但是他唯一能做的工作就只有送報紙，不管怎麼樣，還是得做。

第二天早上，大維開始送報。共有一百份報紙要送，他打算用腳踏車來代步，從離家不遠的街上開始。這是份相當艱鉅的工作。他必須騎在腳踏車上，挨家挨戶把報紙投到門口的階梯上。但是大維瞄準的功力不是頂好，報紙老是卡在樹上，有一次甚至還落在屋頂上。最慘的是，有一次他的報紙居然迎面打中一位老先生的臉，惹來老先生一陣怒斥。於是大維不敢再投擲報紙，只好每到一戶人家，便下車把報紙平平穩穩地送到門口的台階上。這麼做很浪費時間，而且由於天氣太熱，大維開始冒汗，汗水滴滴答答從臉上流下來，滴到背上，甚至連長褲都被汗水浸溼了。

(p.21～p.24)

送報的路線剛好經過愛玫家，大維覺得自己一身狼狽，又臭氣沖天，暗自希望不會碰到愛玫。但卻有一份報紙必須送到愛玫家隔壁！他下了車，走到庭院裡，打算把報紙放好。不料才沒走幾步路，他就聽到一陣吠叫，回頭一看原來是一隻狗，牠對著大維汪汪叫，還露出一口利牙。一向很怕狗的大維忍不住大叫一聲，拔腿就跑，可是狗跑得更快，一邊跑還一邊厲聲咆哮，引得附近屋裡的人們都出來看發生什麼事了。愛玫和她哥哥傑克也出門一探究竟。

（p.25～p.27）

傑克問愛玫：「那不是妳朋友大維嗎？」
愛玫說：「對啊，他在幹什麼？」
那隻狗大口咬住大維那條所費不貲的新牛仔褲，想要把它硬扯下來。大維一直尖叫，想把狗甩開，可是狗咬得可緊了。
狗用力再用力地拉扯大維的褲子，接下來，最糗的事情發生了：牠把大維的牛仔褲扯了下來，然後咬著他的褲子跑了！大維只穿著內褲站在那兒，一臉不敢置信的表情。接著，他又看到愛玫就站在對面，他真的覺得好丟臉，巴不得死了算了。
傑克糗他：「嘿，大維，你的內褲很酷喔！」愛玫則在一旁笑得停不下來。
大維低下頭，嘆了一口氣。他忘了，他穿的是媽媽買的皮卡丘內褲，這是他這輩子最悽慘的一天。
(p.27～p.31)

一個小時後，大維回到家，身上穿著傑克借他的長褲，感覺糟透了。
爸爸問他發生了什麼事，他便一五一十地告訴了爸爸。
爸爸說：「我很遺憾發生了這種事，可是你到底要錢做什麼呢？」
大維決定實話實說，便把他想買情人節禮物送愛玫的事說出來。
爸爸聽完後哈哈大笑：「喔，我懂了！好吧，我就給你買禮物的錢好了。」
大維簡直不敢相信他的耳朵：「真的嗎？我本來以為你不會懂的。」
爸爸說：「我也曾經像你這麼年輕，我還記得那時候的心情。」
大維盯著爸爸的臉，他沒辦法想像爸爸小時候的模樣，不過他很高興爸爸可以了解他的苦衷。他還覺得自己有點蠢，如果早點把事情說清楚，就不會出這麼大的糗，而愛玫也不會看到他的皮卡丘內褲了。
大維嘆了口氣，十三歲的孩子可真不好當，非常不好當。
(p.33～p.37)

全新的大喜故事來囉！這回大喜又將碰上什麼
讓我們趕快來瞧瞧！

Anna Fienberg & Barbara Fienberg／著　Kim Gamble／繪　柯美玲・王盟雄／譯

大喜與奇妙鐘

哎呀呀！
村裡的奇妙鐘被河盜偷走了，
聰明的大喜
能幫村民們取回奇妙鐘嗎？

大喜與大臭蟲

可惡的大巨人！
不但吃掉人家的烤豬，
還吃掉人家的兒子。
大喜有辦法將巨人趕走嗎？

大喜與魔笛

糟糕！走了一群蝗蟲，
卻來了個吹笛人，
把村裡的孩子們都帶走了。
快來瞧瞧大喜是怎麼救回他們的！

的難題呢？

探索英文叢書・中高級

中英對照，每本均附 CD

大喜與算命仙

大喜就要死翹翹了！？
這可不妙！
盧半仙提議的方法，
真的救得了大喜嗎？

大喜勇退惡魔

蜘蛛、蛇和老鼠！
惡魔們絞盡腦汁要逼大喜
說出公主的下落，
大喜要怎麼從惡魔手中逃脫呢？

大喜與寶鞋

大喜的表妹阿蓮失蹤了！
為了尋找阿蓮，
大喜穿上了飛天的寶鞋。
寶鞋究竟會帶他到哪裡去呢？

•中英對照•

探索英文叢書・中高級

波波唸翻天系列

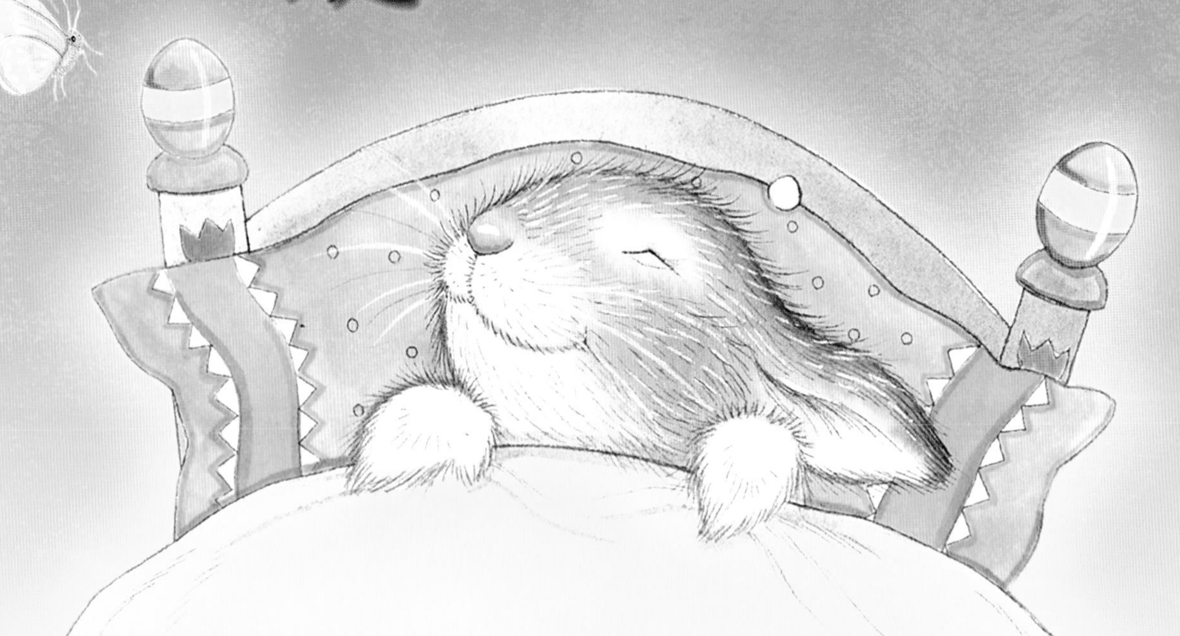

你知道可愛的小兔子也會"碎碎唸"嗎？

波波就是這樣。

他將要告訴我們什麼有趣的故事呢？

波波的復活節／波波的西部冒險記／波波上課記

我愛你，波波／波波的下雪天／波波郊遊去

波波打球記／聖誕快樂，波波／波波的萬聖夜

共9本，每本均附CD

國家圖書館出版品預行編目資料

David the Rebel:叛逆大維打工記 / Coleen Reddy著;
倪靖, 郜欣, 王平繪; 蘇秋華譯.－－初版一刷.－－
臺北市；三民，2002
面；公分--(愛閱雙語叢書. 青春記事簿系列)
中英對照
ISBN 957-14-3660-7 (平裝)

805

© David the Rebel
──叛逆大維打工記

著作人 Coleen Reddy
繪 圖 倪靖 郜欣 王平
譯 者 蘇秋華
發行人 劉振強
著作財產權人 三民書局股份有限公司
臺北市復興北路三八六號
發行所 三民書局股份有限公司
地址 / 臺北市復興北路三八六號
電話 / 二五〇〇六六〇〇
郵撥 / 〇〇〇九九九八──五號
印刷所 三民書局股份有限公司
門市部 復北店 / 臺北市復興北路三八六號
重南店 / 臺北市重慶南路一段六十一號
初版一刷 西元二〇〇二年十一月
編 號 S 85621
定 價 新臺幣參佰伍拾元整
行政院新聞局登記證局版臺業字第〇二〇〇號

ISBN 957-14-3660-7 (平裝)

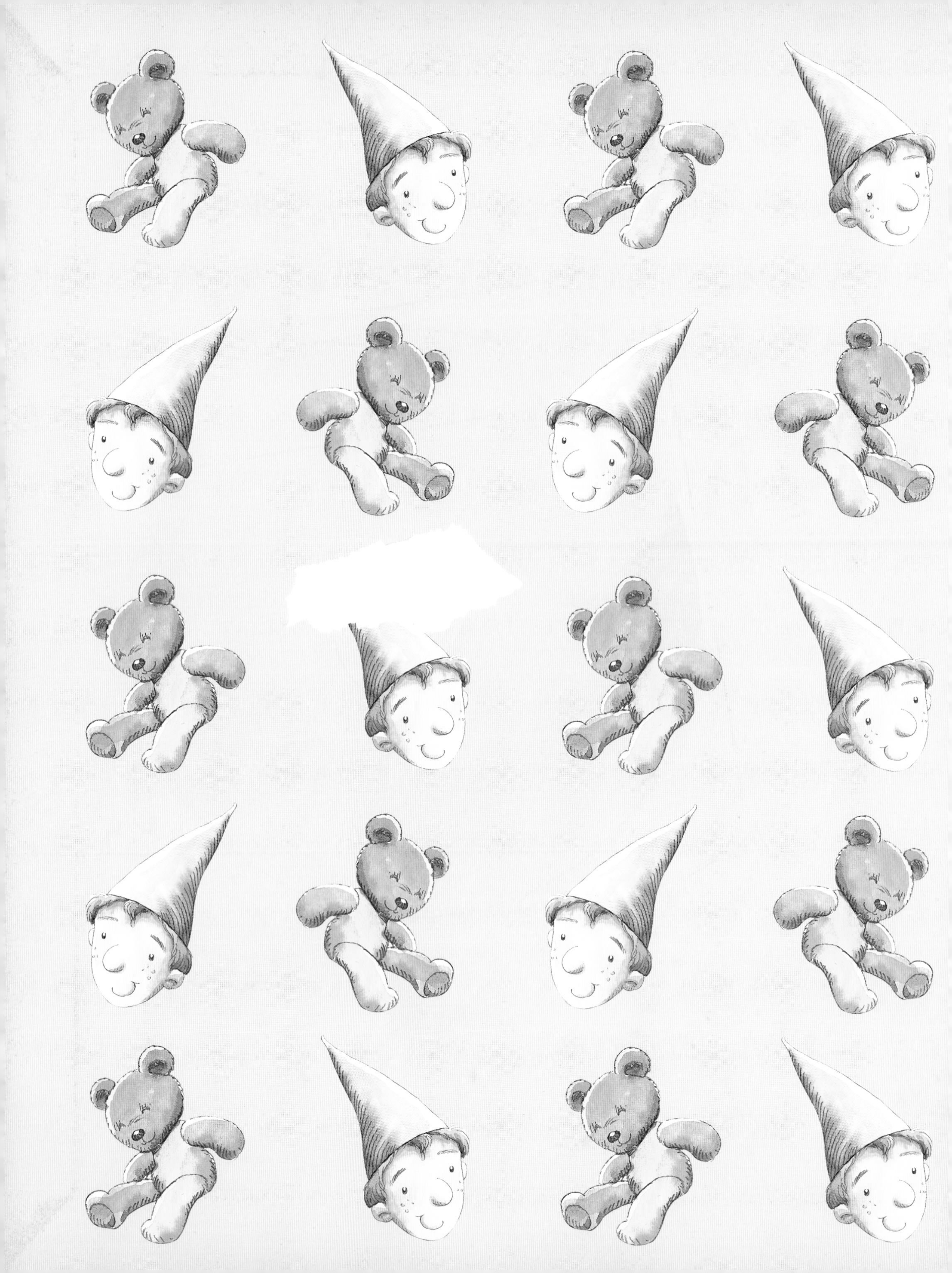